PANDA PANIC

PANDA PANIC
Running Wild

Jamie
Rix

Illustrated by
Sam Hearn

BARRON'S

First edition for the United States published
in 2013 by Barron's Educational Series, Inc.

Text © Jamie Rix 2012
Illustrator © Sam Hearn 2012

First published in 2012 by HarperCollins Children's Books
77–85 Fulham Palace Road
Hammersmith, London W6 8JB

All inquiries should be addressed to:
Barron's Educational Series, Inc.
250 Wireless Boulevard
Hauppauge, New York 11788
www.barronseduc.com

ISBN: 978-1-4380-0308-5

Library of Congress Catalog No.: 2013936281

Date of Manufacture: July 2013
Manufactured by: B12V12G, Berryville, VA

Printed in the United States of America
9 8 7 6 5 4 3 2 1

For Ben, Jack, Charlotte, Jolyon,
Isabel, and Robbie, who at some stage
in their lives have all run around
with a Little Bear behind.

CHAPTER ONE

They were the ugliest bandits that Ping had ever seen—faces as creased as twisted towels and scars as thick as earthworms. They had snatched the Emperor of China from his golden carriage while he was visiting Emperor

Qin's terracotta army at the Great Wall, thrown him across the back of a horse, and were preparing to escape into the hills with their prize. People stood around horrified, not knowing what to do. Only one person could save the kingdom. Ping the Unpetrified! The Emperor's bodyguard! Standing up on his back legs beside the pottery warriors, the panda cub sucked in his tummy, held his breath, and raised his head in a noble, warrior-like way. He was so perfectly camouflaged amongst the statues that the bandits walked right past him without so much as a glance in his direction. That was their mistake.

Ping leaped out behind them.

"Where are you going with my Emperor?" he growled.

"And who are you?" snarled Stinkie McScar, the bandit leader, as he turned around slowly and spat out a tooth.

"The name's Ping!" said Ping. Then with a bloodcurdling wail of "Banshai!" he sprang forward, floored Stinkie with a ninja kick, snatched the Emperor off the horse, and set off running down the Great Wall of China with the bandits giving chase.

"Where are you taking me?" the Emperor screamed as he bounced up and down on the panda cub's back.

"To safety," came Ping's steely reply. "Now be quiet and hold your breath." And with that, Ping leaped off the top of the Great Wall and plunged three hundred feet into the river below. The water was cold and the current strong, but Ping was a powerful swimmer and in less than six strokes he had the Emperor safe on the bank.

"My mustache is wet," said the Emperor.

"Just be thankful you've still got a head to grow one on," said Ping. "We're not out of the woods yet, Your Emperorship."

Screaming loud for all to hear, the bandits burst out of the trees and ran toward them. Ping wrapped his arms around the Emperor's waist and back-flipped onto the top of a mound of dry earth.

"We're safe up here," he said. "Now blow them a raspberry."

"But I'm an Emperor," said the Emperor. "And Emperors must remain dignified at all times."

"Then it's lucky I'm here!" roared Ping, spinning around, wiggling his bottom and

blowing a raspberry at Stinkie McScar through his legs. Angered by the panda cub's insult, the bandits charged, but just as they were within striking distance, Ping grabbed the Emperor for a second time and somersaulted off the mound.

"Hey, ugly muglies," Ping shouted up at the bandits, who were now standing in a huddle on the top, "Check out what's under your feet." As he spoke, the mound collapsed under their weight and the bandits plunged into a nest of deadly termites that quickly gobbled them up.

That was when Ping woke up.

"Oh, fiddlesticks," he groaned, taking

in his surroundings. "Another day, another daydream."

It was first thing in the morning, and Ping was lying on a bed of rhododendron leaves in a clearing in the Wolagong Nature Reserve. Next to him lay his mother, Mao Mao, and twin sister, An, both smiling serenely as they chomped on opposite ends of the same stick of bamboo.

"Bamboo in bed," smiled Ping's mother. "Heavenly. Do you want some, Ping?"

Ping shook his head.

"What were you dreaming about?" demanded his sister. "You were sucking in your tummy and jumping up and down and twirling your arms around like a windmill."

"None of your business," Ping said grumpily.

"You were dreaming about being the Emperor's bodyguard again, weren't you?" she snorted.

"Might have been," said Ping evasively. "I don't see why you think it's so funny."

"Because you're a lazy panda, not a fit,

muscled action hero! The only way you could guard the Emperor is if you wedged yourself into the doorway of his bedroom so that nobody could get in."

"If you must know, I was dreaming that I was actually *doing something* for once."

"Why?"

"Because I'm bored!" he shouted. It wasn't that Ping didn't like eating bamboo, or digging a hole in the forest forty-seven times a day so that he could take yet another poo, or even that he objected to smiling continuously for the visitors' clickety-clack cameras, but when that was ALL he ever did, his life quickly became rather boring.

"I've had an idea," he said, jumping to his feet enthusiastically.

"Oh, here we go," said An with a sigh.

"What do you mean, 'Oh, here we go'? I haven't gone anywhere yet," protested Ping. "If you don't mind me saying so, An, that's a rotten thing for a brother to hear from his sister just after he's woken up."

"It's because you say the same thing every morning," she explained. Then, adopting a look of mock excitement, she mimicked Ping's voice. "'Oooh! Oooh! Oooh! Oooh! An! Listen. I have a completely brilliant idea. I was wondering how you feel about climbing a tree today?'" She stopped imitating Ping and spoke in her own voice again. "The same as I always feel about climbing a tree, Ping. The same as I feel about swimming across a river, or rolling down a hill, or running in a race, or throwing a stick. I would rather I was sitting here eating bamboo with Mommy."

"You'd never make a good adventurer," Ping observed.

"I don't want to be an adventurer," she said. "I'm happy at home."

"As should you be, Ping," his mother interjected. *"A stranger who walks in a strange land knows not where to hide from the toothsome smile of a predator."* Ping had never been able to understand his mother's sayings. It seemed to him that she just picked out unrelated words and arranged them at random into baffling sentences.

"You don't understand what Mommy's just said, do you?" jeered An. "You're trying to look like you do, but you haven't got a clue!"

"Of course I understand," said Ping. "It's got something to do with going on vacation and forgetting your toothbrush… I think."

"Wrong," said his sister, smugly. "It means that I am the clever one and you are not, because I *do* understand it. It means that panda cubs are safer at home, because the rainy season's just finished and the snow leopards are coming down from the mountains looking for food!"

"I'm not scared of snow leopards!" Ping scoffed. "Is that why you won't go exploring with me?"

"Yes," said An. "When I'm at home I know where to hide. And that is why, in case you were wondering, I'm so much better at hide-and-seek than you."

"No, you're not!" said Ping. Then, realizing he could turn this to his advantage, he added, "Prove it!"

An yawned.

"You won't convince me that easily," she said. "Besides, I'm too young and pretty to be a snow leopard snack, but you go ahead if you want to."

Their mother chuckled.

"Nobody's going to be eaten by a snow leopard," she said.

"At least it would be a bit of excitement," Ping replied, without thinking.

"That is a ridiculous thing to say," his

mother sighed. *"The wise panda searches not for what he does not have, but is content with what is his."*

Ping was baffled again and scratched his head.

"Master the art of boredom," she explained further, *"and you will conquer the world."*

"How can you master boredom?" he asked. "Boredom's just boring."

"If you're bored," she said quietly, "it's up to you to go off and find something to do."

"Like what?"

"Like fishing," she suggested.

"Fishing's boring," said Ping.

"Fishing's safe," his mother said.

"So long as you don't fall into the water," snickered An. "Which Ping probably would, because he's as clumsy as a fairy in concrete boots."

"And it is the end of the rainy season, so the river's running rather fast at the moment," said his mother anxiously. "Actually, I've changed my mind, Ping. Maybe fishing's not a good idea. Why don't you ask your best friend, Hui, to play with you?"

Hui was a bright-blue grandala bird who entertained Ping for hours with his exciting stories about flying around the world.

"Because he's busy catching insects for his winter nest," said Ping. "He said I could help him, but I hate bugs. They nest in my fur and tickle me." Ping scratched his nose and tipped back his head to look at the sky. "You know, sometimes I wish I wasn't a panda. Sometimes I wish I was a bird, like Hui, because birds can go wherever they like."

"You can't be a bird," said An, "because birds have a head for heights. You've got a head for basketball."

"I'm not staying here to be insulted," Ping said, standing up in a huff. "And anyway, if my head is the shape of a basketball, yours must be too. So there!"

"Will you two please stop arguing," said their mother. "You can go off and have a silly adventure, Ping, but don't do anything dangerous, make sure you're back for supper, and watch out for snow leopards!"

"Maybe I will and maybe I won't," he grumbled, kicking his way through a bamboo hedge and stomping out of the clearing.

The moment he was out of sight, Ping felt guilty. He shouldn't be speaking to his mother like that. After all, she was only trying to keep him safe. And she had actually met a snow leopard once, so she knew how dangerous they could be. He'd better say sorry—yes, that would be the kind thing to do—maybe not now, though. *After* he'd had his adventure. He'd do it tonight, when he came home for supper.

"Ping."

Ping spun around, surprised to find his sister standing close behind him.

"Promise me," she said seriously, "that whatever it is you end up doing today, it won't be anything stupid!"

Ping laughed at the very idea.

"As if I would," he said. "As if I would!"

Then he disappeared into the bushes to find himself a surfboard.

CHAPTER TWO

Ping had decided to give surfing another try. He was well aware that his last effort had ended rather soggily, with water being squeezed out of his tail and shaken out of his ears at the veterinarian's office, but that was a long time ago. He was two weeks older now and much, much wiser. Besides, he'd done a lot of thinking about what went wrong on that occasion and had decided that it was all the fault of his surfboard— not its rider. He needed a *single* piece of wood instead of a tray made from bamboo poles lashed together—a big, flexible board that could withstand the pressures that a champion surfer would demand from it.

As luck would have it, five minutes later, as he wandered past the tall ranger's office,

he stumbled upon the perfect piece of wood lying across his path. Someone had even customized it for him by painting it bright green. He went to knock on the back door of the office to ask if he might take it, but to his surprise there *was* no door, just a hole in the wall where a door had once been. He waited outside the office for a couple of minutes, but nobody came, so he helped himself and, clamping his new surfboard underneath his arm, he set off for the River Trickle.

When he arrived, he was surprised at how different the river looked. He had never seen it after the rainy season. It was at least six times wider than normal and as deep as the tallest tree in the forest. It rushed past faster than a galloping horse and roared like a cloud full of thunder. Luckily, there was a shallow pool to one side where Ping could warm-up. It was the veterinarian who had taught him how important it was to stretch before physical activity and he started his warm-up by lunging forward on his left leg while touching the ground with the knee of his right leg. After ten seconds of grunting he swapped legs, lunging forward on his right leg while touching the ground with the knee of his left. It was frightfully complicated, and Ping started to get a little confused. When it came to stretching his arms, he couldn't remember if they should be pointing up or down, or whether he should be bending forward or standing up, or whether his feet should be pointing in or out, or whether he should shut his eyes or keep them open.

After five minutes of warming up he was in trouble. Bending at the waist, he had threaded both of his arms between his legs from behind, grabbed onto his ankles, and then tried to stand up. But when he tried to pull his arms back again, they were knotted around his knees. He slowly toppled forward until his forehead was resting on the ground. With his black and white bottom sticking up in the air and his

head curled under his tummy he looked
like a rolled-up pill bug. Now what was he
going to do? Unfortunately this decision
was taken out of his hands, because just
then, with whoops and mocking cheers,
the golden monkeys arrived to poke fun at
poor Ping.

"Oh,
look," screamed
Choo, their oh-so-witty
leader. "A weird new animal's come
to live in the forest. It's a giant black and
white snail." The other monkeys laughed,
while a cocky young monkey named Foo
approached Ping and sniffed him.

"It smells like a panda," he said. "But
it can't be a panda, because pandas only
ever do three things—eat bamboo, poo
forty-seven times a day, and pose for

tourists' cameras—and this one," he said, running his finger down Ping's curved back, "is trying to be a ski slope!"

"You know very well I'm a panda," said Ping.

The monkeys leaped backward on their branches pretending to be shocked.

"A snail that can TALK!" they yelled, bursting into another chatter of laughter.

"Can you un-knot me, please?" Ping asked.

"My pleasure," said Choo, dropping to the ground and delivering a light kick to the panda cub's bottom. Ping rolled forward into the water and uncurled with a splash.

"Thank you," he said, getting to his feet with as much dignity as he could muster. "Now if you'll excuse me, I'm busy."

"You! Busy!" snickered Choo. "The last time I saw a busy panda was *never*!"

"He's busy paddling in the water," snorted Foo.

"Paddling's for babies," Choo roared. "Are you sure you shouldn't be wearing floaties?"

"I am not paddling," said Ping. "I am surfing."

Never before had the monkeys laughed so hard. Their jags of laughter skimmed across the surface of the water like sharp stones.

"We've seen your surfing before, Ping, and there is only one way to describe it," snickered Choo. "It STINKS! Speaking of which, we've got a new name for you— Ping PONG!"

This time the monkeys laughed so hard that they couldn't catch their breath.

Ping had had enough of their jibes. He'd show these stupid monkeys. He waded out into the middle of the river, which was running a whole lot faster than he had thought, and hopped up onto his board. At first he found it almost impossible to get his balance. His arms whirled, his knees buckled, and he wobbled around like a jack-in-the-box on a spring, but then he bent his knees, spread out his arms, and sat back on his haunches—and suddenly he was in control. The current grabbed hold of his board and, with a kick like an outboard motor, whooshed him off downriver.

"Wooooohooooo!" Ping yelled. "I'm doing it! I'm the King of the Surf!" He couldn't see them, but he could hear distinctly that the monkeys had stopped laughing. The river bent sharply to the right, allowing Ping to glance back over his shoulder, where, to his delight, he saw that the monkeys were so shocked to see him surfing that they had fallen out of their trees and were thrashing around in the water trying to get out.

"You should have had some floaties!" hollered Ping. "So long, suckers!" And with a final cry of, "Now you see me, now you don't!" he disappeared around the bend.

The River Trickle twisted and turned through the Wolagong Nature Reserve like a miniature train in a zoo. It carried Ping past all of the other pandas, who seemed strangely unperturbed by the extraordinary sight, as if a panda on a surfboard was something they saw every day. They turned their gentle eyes to watch him pass, but not once did they stop chewing.

Ping floated past the tall ranger, who was searching for something in the garden outside his office. Upon hearing Ping's cry of "Cowabunga!" the tall ranger lifted his head out of a bush and pointed at Ping's surfboard.

"There it is!" he screamed. "There's my back door!"

"Back door!" gulped Ping, looking down at the board beneath his feet. Now that he studied it more closely he noticed that it had a handle and a cat flap. The tall ranger loved his cats.

"And the paint's wet!" shouted the tall ranger.

Nothing I can do about that, thought Ping. *That's the problem with surfing—everything gets wet... my face, my legs, my feet, the board, the paint.* He noticed that the tall ranger was waving a paintbrush. "Oh, I see what you mean!" gasped Ping, lifting up his feet to discover that underneath they were bright green. "You mean the paint's still wet. Sorry!" he cried as he sailed past. "I'll have the door back in two shakes of a cat's tail."

But the cats would have to wait a little longer than that, because Ping's bright-green door-board showed no sign of stopping.

"Look at meeeeeeee!" Ping screamed, punching the air for all he was worth. "I'm living the dream!"

An hour later, swept along by the roaring river, Ping was miles away from home, in a part of the reserve he had never been to before. At last, he was in the middle of his own adventure. It was all he'd ever wanted. And it felt good.

CHAPTER THREE

The farther downriver Ping went, the more he discovered that there was nothing about surfing that he did not love—the spray in his eyes, the wind in his ears, the zip of his board across the water, and the thrill of knowing that at any moment he might wipe out and crash in a waterball of arms and legs. He even liked it when frogs jumped off the bank and joined him on the tall ranger's back door. They would sit at his feet and together they would make up songs about surfing and sing them at the top of their lungs while the water roared around them.

We're brave, we're brave, we're on a wave,
We're wet the whole way through.
We're great, we're great, when we do skate
On rivers deep and blue.
Our floor, our floor, is the ranger's door,
No time to eat bamboo.

The rocks, the rocks scare off our socks,
I really need a poo!

Ping sang the last line on his own. The frogs stopped the moment they heard the words and looked at Ping with their wide mouths wide open.

"That is the rudest thing I have ever heard," croaked a matronly frog called Lu Chu. "What possessed you to sing it?"

"I need a poo," said Ping matter-of-factly. "It's no big deal. We pandas poo forty-seven times a day. We talk about it all the time."

"Well, we DON'T!" harrumphed Lu Chu. "Our best friends are the high-born emperor ducks, and if they were ever to hear us croaking such crudities, they would terminate our friendship immediately!" And with that she belly-flopped into the water and disappeared in a ripple of red rage.

When he wasn't singing with frogs, Ping was making all kinds of other friends. He gave extreme-waterskiing lessons to baby crocodiles by letting them hang onto his tail with their teeth. "There's only one rule," he informed them at the start of each lesson. "No biting!"

He rescued a squirrel from a floating log, skimmed over the backs of water buffalo as they waded across the river in front of him and, with a cry of, "Bullseye!"

he jumped through the body loops of a surprised python while it dangled from a tree.

But by far his favorite friends were the fish, who swam alongside his board and jumped out of the water like hungry dogs leaping for a juicy steak on a hook in a butcher's shop.

"What sort of fish are you?" Ping asked one of them, a cod-faced fellow with whiskers.

"A catfish," the fish replied.

"Does that mean you're half cat and half fish?" inquired Ping. "Does the cat half of you look at the fish half of you and think, 'Gosh! I look delicious. I could happily eat myself with a cup of milk'?"

"Funnily enough, no," said the fish gloomily. "I'm a fish through and through. Are you a pandafish?"

"Don't be silly," said Ping. "I'm a panda through and through. I know it looks like I'm swimming, but actually I'm standing on a surfboard."

"Well, there you are," said the catfish, diving back into the water. "Don't ask such stupid questions!"

"Ignore him," shouted the other fish. "He's been grumpy ever since the day he was spawned. Play with us instead."

For the next hour Ping happily surfed with the fish, until suddenly, not looking where he was going, he ran over a submerged rock. It acted like a ramp and before he knew what was happening his surfboard had taken off. Ping found himself flying through the air in the middle of a flock of chattering parrots.

"It's a flying panda!" they screeched. "Ooh, look at you with your great big arms and your funny flat feet."

"That's not my feet, it's a surfboard," explained Ping. "And I'm not really flying."

But nobody was listening. Parrots love the sound of their own voices, which is why they never stop talking. Regardless of what Ping said they simply carried on squawking.

"Panda bird! Panda bird! We've never seen a bird that's furred!"

Then suddenly a cold shadow fell across the flock, and with a shriek of terror they were gone. For a fleeting moment, Ping's imagination took over. Why would parrots flee in fear of a shadow? What was it in the sky above him—plunging down toward the top of his head—probably with claws? Surely not a snow leopard. No. Even as he entertained this thought Ping realized it was ridiculous. Snow leopards couldn't fly. Then again, neither could pandas. With a big splash that brought him back to his senses, Ping's surfboard reconnected with the water and, steadying himself, he dared to look up. Above him, with a wingspan twice as wide as the stretch of his own arms, was an eagle—a majestic beast complete with hooked beak, razor-sharp talons, and a gimlet eye.

"Don't eat me!" shouted Ping fearfully as the proud eagle leveled out and flew alongside him.

"Eat you?" the eagle sneered. "Why on earth would I want to eat *you*? You're not a fish, are you?"

Ping shook his head.

"It's fish I love," the eagle explained. "I spotted you from a mile up, flying with those noisy parrots and I thought I'd come down and see what you were. What are you?"

"I'm a giant panda," said Ping, just as his board hit a second rock and took off again. The eagle rose effortlessly and stayed in close formation.

"I didn't know pandas could fly," he said doubtingly, looking down his beak at Ping.

"I'm not just any panda," Ping said as he splashed down again. "I'm the fastest panda in the East!"

"Pandas? Fast?" scoffed the eagle. "Don't make me laugh. From what I've seen pandas are the slowest creatures on earth. All you do is sit around all day eating and pooing."

"I'm not doing that now, am I?" said Ping.

The eagle had to admit that he wasn't.

"Come on," pressed Ping, "I bet I'm faster than you."

"That is an absurd notion," the eagle said contemptuously. "That is like saying a two-toed sloth is faster than a four-legged cheetah."

"Then you won't mind having a race," cried Ping, who was always up for a challenge. "Down to the third bend. On your mark, get set, go!"

And before the eagle could make his excuses, Ping shot off down the river, putting clear water between himself and his rival. The eagle gave chase, cutting through the air like an arrow, but the river was running fast and Ping was able to maintain his lead. In fact, Ping noted with alarm, the river was running *very* fast and the current was getting stronger. Much stronger. It felt like he was traveling on a runaway train going downhill. The riverbank flashed past in a blur as Ping hurriedly twisted and turned around the rocks that kept popping up in front of him. He was moving so fast that he could only snatch a quick glance behind him to check on his rival's position. The eagle was struggling to keep up.

"Who's faster now?" Ping screamed, sensing that victory was his.

"You are!" shouted the eagle. "Stop!"

"I'm not falling for that old trick," Ping laughed. "You get me to stop, then fly straight past me. Forget it!" He set his eyes on the finishing post, but the flock of parrots suddenly reappeared and blocked his view. "Out of the way! Winner coming through!" Ping hollered as they hovered in front of him, frantically flapping their wings.

"Turn back," they squawked. "Turn back, you fool!"

"The eagle's put you up to this, hasn't he?" yelled Ping. "He can't win fairly so he resorts to trickery."

The parrots mouthed a reply, but Ping could not hear them over the roar of the river. Its sound had changed. The constant rumble was louder now—deeper and more threatening—and the air was full of tiny drops of water as if it was raining, yet the sky was cloud-free. In a flash, Ping realized what the birds were trying to tell him.

"Waterfall!" he screamed in panic as the current whipped his board around the next bend and revealed, through a cloud of fine mist, a one-hundred-foot-drop into a rockpool bubbling with frothy white water. It was too late to stop. Before Ping had time even to think about saving himself, the current hurled him out into the middle of nowhere. His surfboard dropped out of sight and for one brief, terrifying second, he seemed to hang in midair as if suspended on elastic. Ping had wished for many things in his life, but right now he would have swapped them all for just one—he wished that he'd listened to his mother's warning about not going near the river.

And then the elastic snapped and he went into a freefall.

CHAPTER FOUR

While he was falling Ping must have bumped his head, because when he woke up he had no memory of how he'd ended up where he was. He was lying in the shallows of the riverbank with his head out of the water, resting on a log.

61

He stood up, shook the water out of his fur, and stepped onto dry land. This part of the forest was quite different from where Ping normally lived. The trees were tall and shaded the forest floor, which was as dark and gloomy as an open mouth. Ping shivered. Where was he and what were all those strange noises he could hear? The cry of a bird that sounded like a scream, the plop of a slithering beast as it slipped into the water, the whistle of an eerie wind. One thing was certain—Ping was lost.

"No. Stop! This is stupid," Ping said out loud to himself. "Being scared is getting me nowhere. I wanted an adventure and an adventure I've got—just not the one I was planning to have! No, I shall be brave and walk along the riverbank until I find someone to help me." Ping found that if he talked out loud it made him feel like somebody else was walking alongside

him, and that made everything seem a
little less scary.

As he set off, however, a leaf rustled to his
right. Ping turned his head.

"Who's there?" he cried.

There was no reply, just the sound of
Ping's fur rubbing together as his legs
started shaking. What he wouldn't give
to hear his mother's voice now, even if it
was just spouting one of her silly sayings.
Instead he heard a twig snap and Ping let
out a tiny yelp. He heard footsteps behind
him and, spinning around, he watched
in horror as a shadow crept out from the
forest toward him. What kind of fool was

he? Why hadn't he listened to his mother? Even though it was annoying to Ping at the time, what she said now made a lot of sense. What if a snow leopard had seen him fall over the waterfall and come down from the mountain looking for food? No! No! No! No! No! NO! Ping had to stop these wild and unhelpful thoughts. He wasn't scared of shadows. Shadows were full of nothing and nothing couldn't hurt him. And that was his final word on the matter. He would just walk on calmly, as if nothing was out there. Well, maybe he wouldn't walk. Maybe he'd run. That would be more sensible. Run like the wind and leave this spooky place as far behind him as possible!

"Hello," said a tiny, squeaky voice behind him. "Don't be afraid. I'm only little."

Ping stopped in his tracks and turned to look at where the voice had come from. Standing in a patch of sunlight was a tiny black bear cub. Ping had never felt so silly in all his life. Even if this tiny black bear was to stand on its tiptoes and stretch out both of its arms, it still wouldn't come up to Ping's chest.

"I'm not scared," Ping said, strolling back toward the cub. "I was just going for a run to get a bit of exercise."

"I thought you were running away," said the cub.

"Well, you thought wrong," smiled Ping. "We all make mistakes."

"Did you make a mistake when you tried to swim over the waterfall?" asked the black bear cub. "Did you think you were a penguin?"

"I have never thought I was a penguin," said Ping. "I am the same color, I grant you, but I am a wholly different shape. And I was not swimming, I was surfing." As he said this, Ping's memory came flooding back. "But did I make a mistake when I shot over the waterfall? Yes, I suppose I did."

"I knew that when I watched you fall," said the cub. "I said to myself, 'He didn't mean to do that!' That's what I said to myself. Is your head all right now?"

"Thank you, it is," said Ping, rubbing the bruise behind his right ear. He was touched that the little cub had asked.

"So where is your surfboard?" Now that he had gained Ping's trust the black bear cub had a million questions that he wanted to ask and they tumbled out of his mouth like apples falling from an overturned cart. "Did you really surf on that smashed-up plank of wood? Now that it's broken, how are you going to get home again? Does that mean you'll be living with me for the rest of my life? Do you want to be my friend? How many friends do you have? Is it true that pandas eat bamboo? Why do you eat something that tastes so disgusting?"

Ping could not get a word in and eventually he put his paws over his ears and shouted, "Whoa! You're making my head hurt again."

The black bear cub fell silent.

"Have I done something wrong?" he asked quietly.

"You're asking a lot of questions," said Ping.

"Everyone always says I talk too much and ask too many questions," said the cub. "Do you think I do?"

"I think that you're a very little bear to be out here in this forest on your own," Ping said, realizing that he sounded just like his own mother.

"I'm not scared of snow leopards," said the black bear cub.

"We all say that," admitted Ping ruefully.

"If one came near me I'd bop him on the nose."

"Good for you!" said Ping. "Now, what's your name?"

"Little Bear," said the cub. "I was given that name because I am little and I am a bear."

"It's very well suited," said Ping. "My name is Ping."

"Ping?" said Little Bear, bursting into a fit of giggles. "That's the noise a stone makes when you bounce it off a rock."

"It's also the name of a brave and fearless panda called Ping the Unpetrified!" Ping said briskly, feeling the need to stamp his authority on this friendship early on.

"Who's that?" gasped Little Bear.

"ME!" shouted Ping.

Little Bear beamed up at his new friend.

"I think you're very brave and fearless," he said in awe and wonder.

"That's very kind of you to say so," said Ping. "I try to live up to my reputation."

Ping was used to being small and young and to everyone either ignoring him or making fun of him. So now that somebody was looking up to him and thinking he was marvelous in every way, the attention went straight to his head. He let his tongue and his imagination run away with him.

"I don't suppose you know why I'm called Ping the Unpetrified, do you?" he asked casually. "It's because I'm the Emperor's bodyguard."

"The Emperor?" gasped Little Bear. "Do you mean the Emperor of China?"

"We're very good friends," nodded Ping. "We've eaten deep-fried locusts together, played several games of Chinese Checkers—all of which I've won—and if anyone ever has to stand in as the Emperor's double, they always ask me first."

"Now that you've said that, I can see the likeness," said Little Bear, peering closely at Ping's face.

"I've always had a very regal nose," said Ping, thinking he had probably pushed his luck just a little too far, but Little Bear was much too star-struck to notice the lie. "In fact," Ping continued, "I'm on my way to see the Emperor now."

"Are you? Why?"

"Well, it's top secret so I shouldn't really tell you, but if you promise to keep your lips zipped I suppose I could."

"I promise," said the cub eagerly.

"Then here goes," said Ping. You could practically hear the cogs whirring in his brain as he dreamed up a story to impress Little Bear. "The kingdom is under attack from bandits who want to keep China for themselves. Not just any old bandits, but really ugly ones with faces as creased as twisted towels and scars as thick as earthworms."

Little Bear flinched.

"My auntie looks a bit like that," he said.

"They tried to take the Emperor hostage while he was visiting the Great Wall of China," Ping continued grandly, "but I disguised myself as a terracotta warrior and foiled their plan." Ping had no misgivings about turning his dream into fact. "And now the Emperor's worried that they might try again. His spies have told him that when the bandits attack they will use sharpened bamboo sticks as spears, so I'm the obvious bodyguard for the job."

"Why?" asked Little Bear.

"Because I can eat all the bamboo forests around the Emperor's palace so that there are no bamboo sticks left."

"Because you love bamboo?"

"Exactly," said Ping.

"Gosh," gasped Little Bear. "That sounds like a very important job. So are you going to the palace now?"

"I am," said Ping. "And I'm running a bit late after my accident with the waterfall, so I probably should be on my way."

But Little Bear was not ready to let Ping go.

"Can I come with you?" he begged. "I want to fight for the Emperor alongside you."

Ping could not believe how stupid he had just been. By opening his big mouth and making up a story, he'd got himself into a pickle again. Why did he never learn that sticking to the truth was always the safest option? Now he had to think of another lie to get himself out of the mess created by his first one!

"The thing is..." he said, "there's a minimum height restriction to be a bodyguard and you're just under it."

"I can grow!" cried Little Bear. "Besides, I really hate bandits so that must count for something."

Every barrier that Ping put in Little Bear's way the clever little cub simply swatted away. "Bandits took my daddy and sold him to a cruel circus," Little Bear continued, as a large tear rolled down

his cheek. "And I've never seen him since. So please let me come. We could gather an army of big animals from the forest and all march up to the Emperor's palace together. I'm sure we'd only have to ask. I know lots of big animals who'd listen to your story and gladly fight for the

Emperor, if you'll only let me take you to them."

If Ping allowed Little Bear to tag along, the cub would quickly find out that not only did Ping *not* know the Emperor, but that he had *never* been to the palace and didn't even know where it was—and frankly that discovery would be too embarrassing for Ping to bear.

"The truth is," he said, trying a different approach, "that being a bodyguard is much too dangerous for a little cub like you. Besides, shouldn't you be getting home soon?"

"I should really," said Little Bear.

Ping's eyes lit up. This was his chance to wriggle free from his lie.

"So which way are you going?" he asked.

"Which way are YOU going?" said Little Bear, cleverly throwing the question right back at Ping.

Thinking that Little Bear would live in the forest, Ping pointed in the opposite direction.

"That way," he said. "Downriver."

"Me too!" squealed Little Bear. "We can walk together."

Ping gave up. Little Bear would be hanging around for a little while longer and there was nothing he could do to stop him. Not that Ping particularly minded. He was secretly glad to have company.

They set off along the riverbank toward Little Bear's home. Ping pretended to study the trees so that he didn't have to talk and risk getting himself into more trouble, but Little Bear was too excited about meeting someone who actually knew the Emperor to stay quiet for long.

"Tell me about the Emperor," he asked. "Does he live in a huge palace?"

"I need a poo," Ping said suddenly, disappearing into the bushes for the twenty-sixth time that day. It was an excuse for him to think. Little Bear's questions were proving more and more difficult to answer.

"Well?!" shouted Little Bear, while Ping sat contemplating behind a bush. "Does he live in a huge palace?"

"It's hard to say," Ping called back. "It's not exactly huge, but it's not exactly small."

"What exactly is it, then?" cried Little Bear.

Ping sighed. It was going to be a long day unless he could drag something spectacular from his imagination.

"Give me a minute," he said, "and I'll tell you."

CHAPTER FIVE

For the next hour Ping and Little Bear wandered downriver, climbing over rocks and wading through the shallows. When the water was too deep, Ping gave Little Bear a piggyback, which made the tiny cub squeal with delight. He was full of questions, of course, and didn't stop talking, and Ping eventually decided that it would be simpler just to tell Little Bear what he wanted to hear. After all, he was taking him home and would probably never see him again. And what was the alternative? If Ping was to tell Little Bear that all he really did was eat, sleep, and poo forty-seven times a day, the cub would be gravely disappointed. No. It was kinder to carry on lying. So Ping talked about the fitness training that went into being a bodyguard, and the ceremony at the palace when he was given the job by the Emperor. He talked about learning how to write with invisible ink, how to eavesdrop on bandits using nothing but a seashell, how to make a walkie-talkie out of a bamboo pole, and how to drive a Jeep.

"Incredible!" gasped Little Bear. "But you still haven't told me about the palace. What's it like living there?"

"Well, there's lots of feasting, obviously," lied Ping, "and people dancing in dragon costumes and drinking loads of tea. They like their tea at the palace. That's why the Emperor keeps beavers in the garden, because beavers make the best tea."

"And I bet they're really good at chopping firewood as well," said Little Bear. "Are the clothes beautiful?"

"I've never seen a beaver wearing clothes," said Ping.

"Not the beavers' clothes," said Little Bear. "The courtiers' clothes."

"Beautiful," Ping declared. "There is gold and silver thread everywhere, and not a wooden button in sight, because they are all made from rubies or diamonds. And everyone's wearing bracelets and necklaces and trinkets of all shapes and colors. But the main thing is that around the court you have to look neat."

"Of course you do," nodded the cub. "The Emperor doesn't want to talk to someone who looks like a scarecrow."

"Or someone who's got black currant

juice on his chin," agreed Ping. "And of course when you are sitting at the table you must never burp. That's absolutely forbidden. The Emperor can cut off your head for burping. As for bottom-burping... that's even worse."

"What does he cut off if you bottom-burp?" asked the wide-eyed cub.

"Your bottom," said Ping, "so you can never do it again. And here's a strange one—when you go to the bathroom you're not allowed to go in the forest, you have to sit indoors on a wooden seat with a hole in the middle."

Little Bear wrinkled up his nose.

"That sounds dirty," he said.

"It's not pretty," said Ping. "Unlike the bedrooms."

"They're pretty, are they?" asked Little Bear.

"And comfortable," added Ping.

"Well, they would be," Little Bear said. "Emperors *always* have to sleep on comfortable beds, don't they?"

"That's why his mattress is stuffed with rhododendron leaves," said Ping, unable to stop the fibs from tumbling out. "And he heats his bed with a hot-water beetle. It's the height of luxury. The servants slide a water beetle between the sheets and encourage it to run around until it's hot."

Every time he opened his mouth Ping made his situation worse. There was one point, however, that he enjoyed returning to again and again.

"You have to be exceptionally brave to be a bodyguard," he said.

And each time Ping said it, Little Bear grew more and more impressed by him.

"I think you're very brave," he said. "I wish I was you."

"Thank you," Ping replied graciously. "But sometimes even bravery's not enough. Sometimes you have to be prepared to put yourself in mortal danger to save someone else's life."

Little Bear asked him what the scariest

fight he'd ever had was. Ping rose to the challenge and made up a story about twelve masked bandits scaling the walls of the palace in the dead of night.

"It was my job to scare them away before they could hurt the Emperor," he said. He told Little Bear he had hung upside down off the palace roof, clinging onto the ramparts with nothing but his bare paws, and repelled them with hedgehog bombs, armadillo grenades, flamingo throwers, and anti-bandit mosquito missiles, which he'd thrown down on top of their heads.

Little Bear squealed with excitement.

"Did they fall off their ladders?" he asked.

"They fell in the moat, which I'd filled with specially trained crocodiles," said Ping. "You should have seen the speed with which they jumped out of that water!"

"Wow!" gasped Little Bear. "Twelve masked bandits, specially trained crocodiles, and hanging off the roof by your toes! You are so brave."

Although Ping liked being called brave, the truth was that every time Little Bear said this to him, Ping felt a little bit sadder, because of course he knew that he *wasn't* brave. Yes, he'd surfed down the river, but that was more stupid than brave. He'd never put his life in danger to save someone else—it was all made up. But obviously he couldn't say this to Little Bear without breaking the cub's heart and making himself look stupid. So he didn't.

Instead he offered to show Little Bear how to be a bodyguard and stop a bandit from creeping up on the Emperor.

"I'll be the Emperor's bodyguard," Ping said. "You be the bandit and this katsura tree can be the Emperor. Obviously he tends to move around a bit more than a tree, but you get the idea."

"You won't hurt me, will you?" said Little Bear nervously.

"Why would I hurt you?" Ping asked.

"Because you're a martial arts master and you won't be able to restrain yourself when you catch me."

"My body may be a lethal weapon," Ping said seriously, "but I always keep it firmly under control." And he demonstrated what he meant by shouting "Banshai!" and kicking the tree. Unfortunately, he misjudged the distance between his leg and the trunk, kicked the air, and fell backward into a puddle.

"Are you alright?" asked Little Bear, while Ping lay on his back rubbing his leg.

"Lesson number one," said the panda, trying to cover his mistake. "Always let your opponent think he can beat you so that he drops his guard. *Then* you can attack him. Shall we start?"

Ping and Little Bear played Bandits and Bodyguards all afternoon. They found out many things about each other. Little Bear was good at crawling on his stomach and sneaking up on Ping from behind, but

Ping was equally good at looking between his legs and spotting Little Bear before he could touch him. Little Bear was excellent at jumping on Ping's back and putting his hands over Ping's eyes so that he couldn't see where he was going, but Ping was a master of scratching his back against a tree until Little Bear fell off. Little Bear showed a talent for aerial assault, using vines to swing through

the trees like a monkey, while Ping showed a talent for sitting down and pretending to be asleep when actually he had one eye open. Little Bear discovered that he could run silently on the tips of his claws and make a noise like a bird, which was useful for signaling, while Ping discovered that he could pull in his stomach and hide himself behind a tree. They had a great time, leaping off branches and jumping out of bushes to scare the pants off each other. Eventually, after both of them had collapsed to the ground, weary from so much laughter, Ping finally called it a day.

"It's time to get you home," he said.

"But I don't want to go home yet," Little Bear said. "I'm having too much fun. Tell me more about the Emperor. Please!"

"I've told you everything I know," protested Ping.

"Pleeeeeeeeeeease!" begged Little Bear.

"OK. How about the time I went with him to England to meet a Queen named Elizabeth."

"Yes. Tell me about that," Little Bear cried.

"Well, there's not a whole lot to tell," said Ping, stalling for time while he tried to remember what his friend Jack had told him about London. "It rained cats and dogs all the time and we had to use umbrellas to stop the cats and dogs from landing on our heads. And the Queen had just had some new bamboo blinds put up in the palace, which tasted rather delicious. She was charming as I recall, although she did expect us to bow to her all the time."

"What's bowing?" asked Little Bear.

"It's very dangerous. You don't want to know," said Ping quickly. "It's a bendy sort of a dance thing that needs to be done correctly unless you want to end up at the veterinarian's office."

Little Bear shook his head.

"I don't think I want to do that," he said. "But what about the Emperor—will we have to bow when we meet him?"

"You don't give up, do you?" said Ping.

"Please take me with you!" Little Bear begged. "I've already shown you what a great bodyguard I can be and I've never met an Emperor before, and I bet he'd love to tell me all about *you*—about the brave exploits and heroic feats of his favorite bodyguard."

Ping sighed. He'd let it get out of hand again. Why did he never learn to stop making up stories? One lie was never enough. And it wasn't as if his mother hadn't warned him, either.

One lie, two lies, three lies, four,
Five lies, six lies, seven lies, more.
When a lie gets up to ten,
It won't go back in the box again.

Ping had to be firm with Little Bear.

"You have to go home," he said, trying to sound as grown-up as he could. "Your mother will be wondering where you are."

"She won't miss me. Honestly. I've got tons of brothers and sisters!"

"I'm taking you home," said Ping, ignoring the little cub's pleas. "Now show me where it is."

"Just up here," said Little Bear quietly. "But—"

"No buts!" said Ping. "We've had a great time, but it'll be sundown soon and you have to get home to bed."

"But what about you?" asked Little Bear. "Where will you sleep, Ping? Do you want to come and stay at my house? We could have a sleepover and—"

"I'm afraid I don't have time for sleepovers," said Ping, in his this-is-the-end-of-the-conversation voice. "I have to be at the palace before nightfall."

"Oh," said Little Bear disappointedly. "OK, then. Bye bye, Ping. Have a nice life." And with a sad wave of his little black paw he trundled off into the dark forest, leaving Ping all on his own.

As soon as Little Bear was out of sight, Ping breathed a sigh of relief. Never again, no matter how long he lived, would he ever tell another lie. It was exhausting trying to keep track of what he'd said. He sat down on a rock and rubbed the bottom of his paws. He was tired and hungry. Not only that, but looking around at the forest and not recognizing a single feature, he realized just how far he was from home. The thought made him shudder. He'd never spent a night away from his mother before. He should have taken up Little Bear's offer of a bed. But it was too late now. As the shadows lengthened and the air turned cold, Ping sat on the ground and curled up with his back against the rock. He didn't like being alone. Not only that, but those spooky noises had started up again.

The wind whistled.

The leaves rustled.

The twigs snapped.

Ping gasped, sat up, and opened his eyes wide. Something was out there! It was coming closer! And this time it wasn't Little Bear, because Little Bear had gone home!

CHAPTER SIX

Ping decided that there was only one way to conquer his fear. He would walk on. He felt braver when he was moving, and by singing a song about what a fun adventure he was having, he managed to raise his spirits.

My name is Ping,

Adventuring.

A panda bear,

Without a care!

Oh, this is fun.

There goes the sun.

It's getting dark,

Oh, what a lark!

I am so glad,

I don't feel bad,

That I'm alone,

And miles from home.

He then added some loud whistling to scare away any beasts that might be stalking him. But despite the whistling and the singing, he was still feeling nervous. As his eyes flitted from side to side to check that there wasn't something waiting to pounce on him from behind the bushes, Ping realized that fear was not something he had ever experienced before. Giant pandas did not exactly live life on the edge. There was nothing to fear about sleeping, eating, and going poo forty-seven times a day. Unless you accidentally picked up a snake instead of a stick of bamboo and tried to chew its head off. That would be scary. Or sleeping on a volcano. That would be, too. But, generally, pandas lived a safe life without any nasty surprises. And right now Ping wanted a safe life more than anything else in the world. Seeing his sister again, saying sorry to his mother—anything would be preferable to standing in the middle of this gloomy forest with tree shadows stretching out toward him like ghostly fingers.

My name is Ping,
A fighting king,
A dangerous bear,
So don't you dare!

The sun was starting to set when Ping reached a fork in the track. To the left was a path that continued alongside the river, while to the right was a path that disappeared into the forest. Which one should he take? He couldn't get lost if he followed the river, but lurking in the rock pools along its banks would be thousands of mosquitoes waiting to bite him. The forest, on the other hand, would be mosquito-free, but would also be darker and full of the bad sounds that Ping

did not want to hear. Like that sound he was hearing now. He spun around. Behind him there was an unmistakable sound of dry leaves crunching. Ping strained every bone in his ears. There it was again. He could hear footsteps—*actual* footsteps gathering pace and running toward him!

Help! he screamed inside his head. *Please don't let it be a snow leopard!* And now that

he'd had that thought, he couldn't get the picture out of his head—of sharp teeth and red eyes and hot, steamy breath in his face. There it was! There was its shadow! Spreading out from between the trees like an oozing swamp of molasses, rolling out toward him like a long, black tongue! It was huge! Ping knew that he had told his sister that he wasn't scared of snow leopards, but that was not *now*. Not now when his life was in danger. He turned and ran, his heart thumping in his chest like a war drum. He didn't look where he was going. Anywhere would do. The shadow was big and getting bigger. This was no ordinary snow leopard; this was a *giant* snow leopard that would gobble Ping up like a pistachio nut!

"NOOOOOOOOOOOOO!" he cried as the cold shadow clipped his heels and tripped him up. "LEAVE ME BE!"

"Why?" said a familiar voice behind him. "I thought I was your friend."

Ping was lying on the ground with his face in a puddle of slime. He lifted his head, turned around, and was surprised to see Little Bear standing over him.

"You again!" he exclaimed, wiping the green goo off his forehead.

"That's the second time you've been scared of me," giggled Little Bear. "I'm surprised, with all your combat training."

"Don't be ridiculous!" scoffed Ping. "I knew it was you. I was just playing. Like when we were playing Bandits and Bodyguards. I was seeing if you could catch me, which you couldn't."

"Then why were you screaming 'NOO OOOOOOOOOO!'" asked Little Bear, mimicking Ping's terrified scream.

"You didn't give me a chance to finish my sentence," said Ping. "I was planning to say 'NOOOOOOOOOOOOO! YOU CAN'T CATCH ME!'"

Little Bear thought about this for a moment.

"Then why did you shout 'LEAVE ME BE!' instead?" he asked.

"Because," said Ping slowly, giving himself time to think up yet another excuse. "I was being bothered by a bee and I wanted it to leave me. I'd have thought that was obvious. Anyway, that's quite enough about me," he added, changing the subject to avoid further questions. "What are you doing back here? I thought I sent you home to bed."

"But I don't want to go home," said Little Bear. "I've had a change of heart. I want to come with you! To the palace! To have an adventure! I never do anything fun here. And I've never had a friend before."

"No! No! No! No! No!" Ping said sternly. "I'm happy to be your friend, Little Bear, but you must go home."

Ping suddenly noticed that Little Bear had covered his eyes and appeared to be crying. At least, his shoulders were shaking and his voice was trembling with emotion.

"I can't go home," he whispered. "I lied about the bandits taking my daddy and selling him to the circus."

Ping looked surprised.

"It's worse than that!" blubbed Little Bear. "They took my mommy too!"

"They took your daddy *and* your mommy?" gasped Ping. The shock of such awful news caused Ping to catch his breath. He felt terrible saying what he'd just said.

"So I don't have a home," continued Little Bear, sobbing for all he was worth.

"I'm all on my own."

Ping felt tears welling up in his own eyes. It was the saddest story he'd ever heard.

"And it's so boring being a bear on your own," said Little Bear, raising his sorrowful eyes to look straight at Ping. It was a look that melted Ping's heart. As if hearing the terrible tale about Little Bear's parents was not enough, Ping knew all there was to know about life being boring for bears. He felt Little Bear's pain, and there and then made a pledge never to abandon his little friend again. There was still the matter of how he would deal with his lie about being the Emperor's bodyguard, but Ping couldn't think about that now. Having Little Bear back was all that mattered. And it suited Ping. He too was scared and lonely, and he was secretly delighted to have company again.

"Fine," he said. "Well, you'll have to come with me now as it's too dangerous to send you back. But I don't know what the Emperor will say."

Little Bear smiled, then grinned, then beamed with joy.

"I knew you'd take me back," he said. "You say you're tough, but underneath you're just a great big softie!"

The first thing they needed to do was find somewhere safe and warm to spend the night. Now that there were two of them, Ping was no longer scared and he set off along the shaded path that disappeared into the forest. Little Bear scampered behind, chattering excitedly about what he would say to the Emperor when they met, while Ping gave some serious thought to what he was going to do when Little Bear discovered that there was no Emperor and that his new best friend was a liar.

"I can't let it happen," Ping thought. "I'm going to look like such a fool."

It was this that inspired him to think up believable ways to *avoid* meeting the Emperor. What were his options? He could fall over, pretend to break his leg, and say he couldn't walk any farther, but he'd have to make the broken leg look convincing and that might involve pain. He could go into the forest for a poo and pretend to fall down a big hole that he couldn't get out of. He wouldn't really fall into a hole because that would be dangerous. He'd have to dig a hole first, then climb a tree and throw his voice so it *sounded* like he was in the hole. The problem was, he couldn't throw his voice. No. Far simpler to say he'd just lost his way, but then Little Bear would never believe that, because he thought Ping was perfect and could do no wrong. Eventually, Ping settled on a plan involving memory loss. When they didn't find a palace in the morning he would pretend to have banged his head in the night and lost his memory, which, amongst other things, had left him not knowing his own name, not knowing the words for frogs, fish, and flowers, and not knowing directions to the Emperor's palace. It wasn't a great plan. In fact it wasn't even good, but it was the only one Ping had and it would have to do.

"Look!" shouted Little Bear all of a sudden. The shrillness of his voice snapped Ping out of his daydream. "The palace!"

Ping shook his head in disbelief.

"The what?!" he said.

"Through those trees," cried Little Bear. "The Emperor's palace!"

CHAPTER SEVEN

Little Bear was not wrong, or rather, Ping did not know whether he was or not. He could see several buildings through the trees, arranged on either side of a muddy street that opened out after fifty feet or so into a large square where a number of market stands were arranged in a circle. The buildings were all built from wood and painted in bright colors—reds, greens, blues, and yellows—and all of them had thatched roofs and smoking chimneys. Was this really the Emperor's palace? For all Ping knew, it might be. It was not exactly big, but it was not exactly small, either. Just as he'd described it. The truth was, Ping was completely flummoxed. If this was the palace, had he just made it appear out of his imagination? That wasn't possible, was it? But there was no doubt that he HAD been thinking about the Emperor's palace just before Little Bear had shouted, "Look!" So what was it? The Emperor's palace or somewhere else? How was he supposed to know? He'd never been to either. He'd spent all his life at home.

Meanwhile, Little Bear was having no such doubts. He had rushed through the trees and was standing in the clearing on the other side, admiring the buildings.

"You're so clever, Ping!" he squealed. "I knew you knew the Emperor and now I'm going to know him too!"

In truth it was just one of the villages in the nature reserve, so there was absolutely no chance of meeting an Emperor, but Ping didn't know that. As far as Ping was concerned, if his lie was not to be exposed, he had to keep Little Bear believing that the Emperor might appear at any moment.

"This way," he said breezily. "And don't forget your manners."

The sun was still dropping in the west as Ping and Little Bear walked up the street toward the square. This meant that their shadows were huge—they spread up the road in front of them and fell across the path of a small boy who was running home. As their shadows plunged his world into darkness, he stopped running and screamed.

"Giant bears! Run for your lives! The giant bears have come!" And bursting into tears he ran wailing into the nearest house.

At first Ping looked surprised, but then noticing that Little Bear was watching him for a reaction, said, "You see? They know who I am and run in terror before me!"

Little Bear shook his head in disagreement.

"I think he saw our big shadows on the ground and thought that we were both big," he said. "What a silly boy. We're not giants, we're just little cubs."

Of course! thought Ping. *That's why Little Bear's shadow had looked so big and scary in the woods before.*

Ping could not believe that he had been such a fool. It wasn't as if he didn't know that when the sun was low in the sky it made shadows larger. After all, his mother had always told him that *a shadow is only as frightening as the mind that imagined the shadow-maker.* And she was right. Ping had a very active imagination and had envisioned giant snow leopards where none had ever existed.

No longer scared, Ping renewed his efforts to convince Little Bear that he really was a bodyguard.

"Shall I let you in on a secret?" he asked.

Little Bear loved secrets almost as much as a clawful of honey.

"When our long shadows fell across that boy's path—I planned that," said Ping.

"Did you?" gasped Little Bear. "Why didn't you say so sooner? That's so embarrassing. There was me telling you about the sun and long shadows on the ground and you knew all along."

Ping smiled and continued bluffing.

"I'm afraid I did," he said. "As the Emperor's bodyguard it's important that I keep the people a tiny bit afraid of me so that they don't get any ideas about attacking the Emperor."

"That's brilliant," said Little Bear.

"As my mother always says," said Ping, "*a wise bear fights with his brain as well as his body.*"

"I'd like to meet your mother," said Little Bear.

"One thing at a time," chuckled Ping. "Let's see if we can find the Emperor first."

As they walked into the village, Little Bear swung his hips like a cowboy and narrowed his eyes to make himself look mean.

"I'm going to enjoy being a bodyguard!" he growled under his breath.

The villagers must have heard him, because suddenly they all fled, shouting out, "We'll be back with reinforcements!"

"What are reinforcements?" asked Little Bear.

"I don't know," said Ping. "It sounds like something to hold up your pants. Where are you going?"

Little Bear had spotted something in the square.

"Look!" he cried, running up to the unmanned market stands, which were laden with fruit, vegetables, and meat, fine clothes embroidered with silver thread, and glittering trinkets studded with semi-precious stones. "It's just like you said the palace would be!"

"Gifts from the Emperor!" explained Ping, unable to believe his luck. Wherever they were, this place was backing up his story nicely.

Little Bear was hungry and clambered up onto one of the food stands. He sat down, grabbed some fruit, and started to eat it greedily. 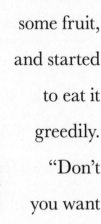 "Don't you want anything?" he asked Ping, the corners of his mouth oozing with the juicy flesh of a pear.

"I'm not really a fruit lover," admitted Ping.

"I could get you some bugs," said Little

Bear helpfully. "If we can find rotting garbage nearby there's bound to be some moldy maggots we could share."

Ping clutched his stomach and shuddered.

"No bugs!" he said quickly.

"Then no bugs it is," said Little Bear, tossing a peach into the air and catching it in his mouth. "Can *you* do that?"

"No," said Ping. "I can toss a stick of bamboo in the air like a cheerleader's baton if you'd like to see that?" But before he could demonstrate, his stomach rumbled loudly and the search for a bamboo baton was overtaken by the search for a bamboo meal. "If you'll excuse me," he said to Little Bear, "I need a little snack. And then, who knows, I might dig myself a hole and have my forty-second poop of the day."

A few minutes later, while squatting over his hole in the woods, Ping looked candidly at his situation. For the last few hours he had been bending over backward trying not to disappoint Little Bear by shattering the image he had of Ping as a hero. Well, maybe now Little Bear didn't need to find out that Ping wasn't the Emperor's bodyguard. Ever since they'd come across the village, Ping's luck had changed. Far from his lie being exposed, it had been backed up time and time again. Maybe his mother was wrong. Maybe sometimes lies could turn out to be true.

And it was in that frame of mind, with a confident swagger to his step, that Ping strode back into the village, believing that anything he said would eventually come true.

CHAPTER EIGHT

By the time Ping got back to the village it was getting late.

"Shall we find somewhere to sleep?" he asked.

"Ooh, yes. Let's sleep in the palace," squealed Little Bear. "Can we, Ping, please? I've always wanted to sleep in a fancy place!"

"I don't see why not," said Ping, looking around for a house that might pass for a palace. "Over there," he said, pointing to the largest house in the village, which was the only one to boast a veranda as well as a front door.

Little Bear was all for just barging straight in, but Ping had been taught to knock before he entered somebody else's house. He held Little Bear back by the scruff of his neck while he waited for someone to open the door. When nobody came, he and Little Bear walked round to the back of the house.

"Why?" asked Little Bear impatiently.

"Because you don't go bursting into a palace without being announced," Ping said. "For all we know the Emperor may be outside in the yard playing croquet."

He wasn't. The backyard was deserted except for a clothesline filled with clothes, a garden rake standing upright in a vegetable patch, and a rocking chair sitting on a small patio made from concrete slabs.

"You know what these are, don't you?" exclaimed Little Bear, rushing forward and jumping up to reach the flapping material. "The Emperor's clothes!" He caught hold of a T-shirt and pulled it down on top of his head. Standing up, he tugged his legs through the arm holes, tied the bottom around his stomach and then, to lend himself an air of importance, borrowed a pair of stripy socks off the line and popped them onto his ears.

"That looks fun!" cried Ping, joining in the game. Now that there was nobody around, Ping's bravery knew no bounds. He grabbed a flowery dress from the clothesline and threw it around his shoulders with a flourish. "This is the Emperor's cape," he declared. "And this—" he reached up for a pair of white underpants and tugged them down over his head "—is the Emperor's crown!"

Then he pulled the rake from the soil and sat down in the rocking chair. "Behold!" he said. "The Emperor is sitting on his throne holding his ceremonial trident."

"Greetings, Your Emperorness," said Little Bear, dropping to his knees. "Shall I kiss your feet?"

"That would be nice," said the Emperor. "And make sure you give them a good lick while you're down there, because I haven't washed them for a week."

"Ugh!" spat Little Bear, leaping up and pretending to be sick.

"Who dares to disobey the Emperor?" roared Ping.

"Me," said Little Bear. "Please don't chop off my head."

"I very well might!" Ping roared. "It depends who you are."

"I'm your bodyguard," said Little Bear,

running over to the vegetable patch and pulling up a carrot. "And today I shall be protecting you with this orange sword."

"It looks delicious," said the Emperor. "But tell me, bodyguard, who exactly are you protecting me from?"

"Bandits!" said Little Bear. "If they so much as look at you in an evil way I shall poke them with this until they run away or get carrot poisoning, whichever is the soonest."

"Well, I'm glad you're here," said the Emperor, "because I'm just about to go to sleep and you and your carrot can protect me while I'm down for the count."

"Consider it done!" shouted Little Bear,

jumping to attention and poking himself in the eye with the carrot.

Snapping out of character, Ping leaped up off the rocking chair.

"Are you alright?" he asked with genuine concern.

"Just a carrot in the eye," said Little Bear bravely. "Nothing us bodyguards aren't trained to cope with. Now, about that sleep."

Ping resumed his position on the Emperor's throne and closed his eyes so that the game could continue.

"Only wake me if there's an emergency," he said in the voice of the Emperor.

"Wake up!" shouted Little Bear.

"What is it?" cried Ping.

"An emergency!" yelled Little Bear. "We're under attack from bandits. Leave it to me, Your Sleepiness." And with that, Little Bear flung himself onto the ground and rolled around with an imaginary bandit, stabbing at thin air with his carrot. After several forward rolls, a couple of back flips, and a great deal of grunting, Little Bear lay exhausted in front of Ping's throne. The carrot was hanging limply from his paw, snapped in half.

"Thank you," said the Emperor. "My body has never been so well guarded. And now I shall reward your bravery by making you a knight. Kneel before me." Little Bear did as he was told, while Ping rose from his throne and laid the rake across Little Bear's shoulder.

"Arise, Sir Little Bear," Ping declared. "You have saved the Emperor's life, and for such loyal service I gift you all of the land that you see before you."

"The whole yard?" gasped Sir Little Bear.

"Including the vegetable patch," said Ping the Emperor. "Grow your vegetables wisely, Sir Little Bear, and may your leeks never wilt!"

By now Little Bear was giggling so much that tears were running down his cheek.

"You make a very good Emperor," he snorted.

"And you make a very good body-guard," Ping laughed back. "And now all that remains for you to do is to bow to your Emperor and then you can run along."

"But I don't know how to bow," said Little Bear. "You haven't taught me how to do that yet."

"It's simple," said Ping. "Watch me." He waved his arms and legs, turned upside down so that the pants dropped off his head, and wiggled his bottom in the air. Little Bear copied Ping exactly and fell flat on his face.

They decided to go inside so that Little Bear could lay down and see for himself how an Emperor lived. Ping had enjoyed playing in the yard so much that he was in a careless mood and forgot to knock on the back door. He gave it a push and it swung open with a creak.

There was nobody there.

The room had a large bed pushed against one wall, a table in the middle surrounded by four wooden chairs, and a square box on legs in the corner facing an old sofa.

"This is what Goldilocks must have felt like when she walked into the bears' empty house," giggled Ping. "She could try out everything and nobody could stop her." He looked at Little Bear, who appeared to be having exactly the same thought as he was, and their faces exploded into mischievous grins. First they tried the bed, bouncing as high as they could on the mattress to see who could touch the ceiling first. Next they tried the saucepans in the kitchen, pushing them down on their heads until they looked like knights' helmets. Then, using cutting boards as shields and chairs as horses, they did a bit of jousting. Finally, they tried the shower, and took turns pretending to be mermaids washing their hair in a tropical storm. They dried themselves on the bath mat and went back into the sitting room so that Little Bear could take another look at the wooden box in the corner.

"What is it?" he asked inquisitively.

Ping prodded the glass window on the front of the square box.

"My friend Hui once told me that humans are fond of keeping fish behind glass windows," he said.

Little Bear peered through the glass until his eyes were sore, but did not see any fish.

Meanwhile Ping, puffed-out from all the fun, slumped onto the sofa and accidentally sat down on a small, hard object covered in buttons. As he did so, the square box lit up and loud music blasted out from either side. Standing so close, Little Bear was taken by surprise. He jumped backward and scrambled behind the sofa to hide from the noise.

"What is it?" he cried.

"Some sort of magic box," gasped Ping as the black screen disappeared and was replaced by a picture of a long-haired rock band playing music on a stage.

"They're very small men, aren't they?" said Little Bear, squinting at the screen.

"I expect they have to live inside the square box to stop other people from treading on them," said Ping.

"You could squash all of them with one paw," observed Little Bear. "Imagine how small I'd be if I lived in there!"

"No bigger than a teardrop," laughed Ping.

"Or an ant's kneecap!" shouted Little Bear.

"Or a hair in the nose of a toad!"

Jumping off the sofa to high-five Little Bear's paw, Ping suddenly noticed that something strange was happening to his hips.

"What are you doing?" Little Bear asked nervously.

"I don't know," replied Ping. "It's like something's taken over my legs. They're wobbling and shaking all on their own."

"And your arms are whirling like dragonflies' wings!"

"So are yours!" cried Ping.

"I know," said a shocked Little Bear. "What's going on?"

"It's the music coming from the square

box," shouted Ping. "I think it's got into our bodies and is making them move."

"Are we possessed by evil spirits?" wailed Little Bear.

"I don't think so," yelled Ping, flinging his arms above his head and kicking up his heels. "I think what's happening to us

is what is known as… DANCING!" And he shimmied his waist until his stomach started to ripple. Casting their fear aside, the two bears gave in to the music and jiggled and gyrated across the floor as if they were hopping around on hot coals. It was only when Ping injected some fast turns and a full spin that they started to lose their balance. They crashed into each other and collapsed in a heap on the floor.

As they did, the door to the Emperor's palace crashed open and some of the men who had run away earlier to get reinforcements burst into the room. Ping and Little Bear looked up, their eyes wide with horror.

"Bandits!" shouted Ping. "Real bandits!"

Little Bear shot Ping a reckless look. Then leaping from the floor like a bear possessed, he screamed the scream of a wild warrior charging into battle, and head-butted the first man in the stomach. The blow lifted him off his feet and knocked him backward into the men behind him, who went down like a line of dominoes.

"Come on, Ping!" roared Little Bear, his voice pumped up with nervous energy. Eager to prove that he had what it took to be a bodyguard, Little Bear was up for a fight, but Ping grabbed hold of one of his arms and dragged him away.

"Quick!" he urged. "Out the back."

"Aren't you going to fight them?" said Little Bear, surprised. "There're only five of them. You've fought many more than that."

"Later!" shouted Ping. "First things first. RUUUUUUUUUUUUUUUUUN!!!!!"

And with ear-socks flapping, pants unraveling, and flowery dresses knocking over precious vases, they ran for the door. They ran as fast as their furry legs could carry them. They ran for their lives!

CHAPTER NINE

Clothes fluttering and arms waving, Ping and Little Bear burst out through the back door and rushed into the backyard like a couple of ghosts. They stumbled on the uneven ground as they glanced over their shoulders to see if they were being followed. Not yet. But from inside the house they could hear the men shouting, "Take your boots out of my ear and go after them!"

"This is such fun!" squealed Little Bear, jumping up and down.

"It won't be if they catch us," said Ping. "That way!"

They set off back toward the forest, scampering as fast as they could go on all fours. Ping's heart was thumping. Little Bear was too young to know what damage a bandit could do, but Ping had been told time and time again that if ever he saw one he should not stop to think, he should just run.

By the time the bandits had untangled their arms and legs and left the house through the back door, Ping and Little Bear were safely out of sight. They were hiding in the forest trying to catch their breath. Little Bear was still overexcited and giggling at the thrill of it all.

"If you hadn't been there, Ping," he gushed, "I would never have been so brave."

But Ping was not laughing. When he'd left home looking for adventure this was not what he'd had in mind. He'd promised his mother that he wouldn't do anything dangerous and he'd meant it. Now his recklessness had nearly got both of them captured, and Ping could not see what was funny about that.

"I may have been there," he said, "but I wasn't much use."

"You're my hero," cooed Little Bear. "You gave me courage."

"I gave you nothing," said Ping glumly, "except a lot of hot air!" The fun had been knocked out of him and Little Bear did not understand why.

They took off their borrowed clothes and for the next few minutes sat in awkward silence. As the sun dipped lower in the sky, Little Bear wondered what he'd done to offend Ping, and Ping wondered how he was ever going to let Little Bear down by telling him the truth. Eventually Ping said, "I'm hungry," and stood up.

Desperate to please Ping, Little Bear scuttled over to a large bolt hole that had been dug out of the soil by a badger, and stuck his paw inside.

"There are some delicious grubs in here," he said, digging at the mouth of the hole, trying to widen it.

"I'll never fit in there," said Ping. "And anyway, I've already told you I hate bugs. I only like eating bamboo. Back at home, that's all I do, apart from sleeping and taking a poo forty-seven times a day."

"All you do?!" said Little Bear. "What about being the Emperor's bodyguard?"

Ping couldn't be sure, but it sounded as if Little Bear was starting to question his story.

"There's that too," he said quietly. "I'm just going to grab myself something to eat. I'll be back in a minute. Are you OK?"

"Don't worry about me," said Little Bear. "I'll be fine."

Ping picked himself a fresh bamboo cane, slumped down against a tree stump, and tore off the leaves with his teeth. He was angry with himself for being so weak. He had told a big lie once before, when he'd informed the international pandas who visited Wolagong that he was a skirt-wearing, plate-spinning, bamboo-cooking, classical bagpipe-playing Winter Olympian, who also happened to be a part-time dragon-fighter. Admitting to this lie had been so embarrassing that he'd sworn never to tell another lie again. And now look what he'd done—he told Little Bear that he was the Emperor's bodyguard, a fearless fighter who wrestled bandits, and single-handedly defeated China's enemies! Only bad things could come of Ping's stupidity. When Little Bear found out the truth, he'd think that Ping was ordinary and boring, and wouldn't want anything more to do with him. It was time for Ping to face up to a few hard facts—he could no more be a hero than he could fly.

Suddenly he heard a cry from the spot where he'd left Little Bear.

"PING!!!! HELP!!!!"

There was a terror in the voice that tore at Ping's heart. He sprang up onto all fours as if struck by a bolt of lightning and, dropping his stick of bamboo, sprinted to Little Bear's rescue. But as he brushed aside the branches and crept into the clearing, he saw a sight that made his blood run cold. Digging out the entrance to the bolt hole, inside of which Little Bear had taken refuge, was a snow leopard! Not a shadow of a snow leopard. A *real* snow leopard, with *real* claws and teeth. It was knocking out clumps of earth and making the hole bigger with each swipe of its paw. It would not be long before it reached Little Bear, and when it did—Ping could not bear to think of losing his friend. But what could he do? A giant panda's instinct when confronted by a snow leopard is to panic. Ping was no exception.

"Flipping flipflops!" he screamed under his breath. "What's the plan, Ping?" He didn't have an answer. His mind had frozen.

"Piiiiiiiiiiiiiiiiiiiiiiiiiiiiiiiiiiiiiiiiiiiiiing!" came the muffled cry from down in the hole. "Save me!"

Come on, Ping! This isn't a game. Snap out of it! What would his mother do in these circumstances, he wondered? She'd attack. She'd protect her children. She'd rush in without a thought for her own safety. Ping wanted to do the same, but his head was *full* of thoughts for his own safety— hundreds of them, in fact. And it was these thoughts that were stopping him from jumping in and saving his friend. His heart was telling him to fight, but his head was telling him he couldn't win.

STOP PANICKING, PING!!!!

Ping grabbed hold of his head and held it still. If Little Bear was to stand a chance of being saved, Ping had to take a deep breath, suck the sense back into his head, and think.

He didn't know what made him look down at the ground, but he did. And when he saw the long shadows that were being cast by the trees and recalled his own saying that *a wise bear fights with his brain as well as his body*, it was but a short leap to a brilliant plan. Why he hadn't thought of it before was a mystery to Ping. But he'd thought of it now and that was all that mattered.

Ping gathered up every trace of bravery in his body by pulling in his stomach and puffing out his chest. Then he tiptoed forward with great care and positioned himself between the setting sun and the snow leopard. In the low, slanting sunlight, his shadow stretched and lengthened and fell across the back of the beast's head. The snow leopard stopped digging and pricked up its ears, aware that some huge creature—if the size of its shadow was anything to go by—was standing directly behind it. Ping filled his lungs and roared, as deep a roar as ever was heard in the forest. "ROOOOOOOOO OOOOOOOOOAAAAAAAAAAA OOOOOOORRRRRRRRRR RRRRRRR!!!!!!"

From the depths of his stomach to the tips of his lips, his body vibrated with the terrifying noise. In its mind's eye, the snow leopard imagined a giant bear behind it and, without looking around, took flight. It rushed away with its tail between its legs and didn't stop running until it was safely hidden in its cave where the giant bear could not reach it.

It had been a bold and brave deception and Ping had triumphed. He rushed to the mouth of the bolt hole and, ignoring the bugs and insects that scuttled across his arms and legs, kicked and scraped a path out of there. Little Bear flew out of the hole and flung his arms around Ping's neck.

"You saved me! You saved me! I knew you would!" he cried. "You scared away the snow leopard and saved my life." They held paws and danced around in a circle, while words continued to pour out of Little

Bear's mouth like a waterfall bursting out of the side of a mountain. "I called your name knowing that you'd come. There was a moment when I thought you might not, but then you *did*. And then you were so brave. You really did it, Ping. No wonder the Emperor chose you to be his bodyguard!"

Ping stopped dancing, but held onto Little Bear's paws.

"I need to talk to you about that…" he said sheepishly, shuffling his feet and sighing the sigh of a panda with the weight of the world on his shoulders. "You might like to sit down."

"No, thank you," said Little Bear. "What's wrong?"

"Well… it's… erm… it's…" Ping was having difficulty forming a sentence. "… None of it's true," he said eventually. "I'm not the Emperor's bodyguard."

"Oh," said Little Bear slowly as the bombshell hit home. "Is this a joke?"

"I wish it was," said Ping.

"But you do *know* the Emperor?"

"Not personally. I know OF him, but we've never actually said hello." Ping couldn't bring himself to meet Little Bear's eyes. He could hear the disappointment in his friend's voice—he didn't need to see it in his face as well. So it came as something of a surprise when Little Bear began to laugh. A light tinkling laugh that wasn't judgmental at all.

"You really are good at telling stories!" he said. "I mean I was completely taken in. Even when we went to the Emperor's palace I kept expecting the Emperor to walk in."

"I don't think it was a palace," said Ping.

"But it must have been," said Little Bear. "A place that fancy could only belong to royalty. It had a square box, chairs, a bed with a mattress, everything!"

"It looked fancy," admitted Ping, "but when those bandits came back, I realized it was just an ordinary house with ordinary people who were scared of bears."

Little Bear paused.

"What else have you told me that's not true?" he asked.

"Well, you know my crown..." said Ping.

The memory of it brought a smile to Little Bear's lips.

"What about it?"

"It wasn't a crown at all," Ping said seriously. "It was a pair of underpants!" Which made both of them fall on the floor with laughter.

It turned out that Little Bear was so in awe of Ping's storytelling skills that he asked his friend to teach him his secret.

Ping beamed with pride.

"You mean you still want to be my friend?"

"Of course I do," said Little Bear. "Why wouldn't I? This has been the best day of my life!" He flung open his arms and hugged Ping's waist. "In fact, all I want to do is take you home and show you off to my mom and dad."

Ping paused to consider what he'd just heard.

"I thought you said your parents were captured by bandits and sold to the circus," he said.

Now it was Little Bear's turn to look ashamed.

"Oh, yes... I forgot I'd said that," he said guiltily. "I don't normally tell fibs, but when you sent me home to bed I didn't have a choice. I mean, I only said all that sad stuff about being an orphan to make you take me with you. I made it all up. Are you very angry with me?"

Ping smiled.

"How could I be angry with my best friend?" he said. "Come on. It's late. Let's get you home before your mom has a fit."

Then they raced each other through the forest and reached Little Bear's home just before their shadows disappeared into the darkening night.

CHAPTER TEN

When Little Bear walked out from between the trees, his family went bananas. His brothers and sisters were the first to reach him, followed closely by his mother and father, and less closely by his aunts, uncles, grandparents, cousins, and a ring-tailed lemur named Arthur who had lived with the black bears for the past three years.

"Where have you been?" his mother screeched as she gathered her baby into her arms.

"Having an adventure!" Little Bear replied, his voice muffled by his mother's armpit. "And this is the bear who saved my life."

The family now noticed Ping for the first time.

"You're a panda," said Little Bear's father.

"Yes," said Little Bear. "And not just any old panda, either. Meet Ping the Unpetrified! He saved me from a snow leopard."

The family was very interested in the details of how Ping rescued their precious son—so much so that Ping was tempted to spin them a big lie to make himself sound even more heroic. But, catching himself just in time, he stopped making up the story and told it like it was instead. He told them about using his long shadow and his loudest roar to trick the terrified snow leopard into believing that he was a giant. And everyone agreed that Ping was incredibly brave.

"A real hero," said Little Bear's mother. Then she turned to Little Bear and picked him up in her arms, squeezing him until he squeaked. "And you too," she said with pride in her eyes. "My brave little soldier!"

Watching Little Bear cuddle his family suddenly made Ping feel rather sad. Not for Little Bear, but for himself. He missed his own family and wanted to be with them.

Little Bear's mother noticed that Ping had suddenly gone quiet.

"Are you feeling homesick?" she asked. "Where did you say your home was, Ping?"

"I don't know," he said with tears in his eyes. "I mean, I know it's upriver, but I don't know how far. I was traveling so fast on my surfboard that I forgot to count the trees."

Just then he looked up to see the shape of a big bird silhouetted against the moonlit sky. "Panda-bird!" it squawked from on high. "Is that you? I thought I'd never see you again after you shot over that waterfall."

Ping's heart skipped a beat. It was the golden eagle that had raced him earlier.

"Yes, it's me!" he cried, jumping up and down and waving his arms with joy.

"Don't move," the eagle yelled. "I've got someone up here who wants to see you."

As the eagle spoke, a second bird flew alongside, only this bird was much

smaller with feathers that glistened in the moonlight.

"Ping!" it yelled. "Where have you been!"

The weary panda cub recognized the voice instantly.

"Hui!" It was his friend, the grandala bird, who had come to take him home.

After Ping had given Little Bear a hug and promised to come back to see him soon, and then given him another hug, and then waved to the whole family, and then gone back to Little Bear for a third hug, Hui called time on the goodbye.

"Come on, Ping. It's not as if you're never going to see each other again."

"He's right," said Little Bear's mother. "Your mother will be worrying, Ping. Now, GO!"

Which was just the motivation Ping needed to send him on his way.

It was a long walk home. For Ping, that is. Hui simply sat on the panda cub's shoulder and went along for the ride.

"Are we almost there?" Ping asked, after ten minutes on the trail.

"No," said the grandala bird. "It's going to take all night."

"Isn't it a bit dangerous walking in the dark?" said Ping.

"I thought your middle name was danger," chuckled Hui.

"I don't think I've got a middle name," Ping observed after a moment's reflection. "If I did have one I'd like it to be Brad. Sounds like the sort of person an

Emperor would take on as a bodyguard, doesn't it?"

"You don't give up, do you?" said Hui, as Ping stumbled on a rock.

"I told you it was dangerous walking in the dark," he complained.

"Wait here," said Hui, taking off from Ping's shoulder and flying into the trees.

"Where are you going?" shouted Ping. "Don't leave me here on my own in the middle of a dark forest!"

"Back in a sec!" hollered Hui. "Besides, now that you've scared a snow leopard I thought you were brave."

Hui had a point. Ping decided to test himself to see if he *was* brave. He cupped his ears and listened for spooky forest sounds. And even though he heard the wind whistling, the leaves rustling, and the occasional twig snapping, he discovered that they didn't scare him quite as much any more. Besides, he wasn't alone for long. Hui returned ten seconds later with a swarm of fireflies.

"To light our passage," he explained. "Shall we continue on home?"

They arrived home just as dawn was breaking over Mount Tranquil. An ran to greet Ping as he walked into the clearing, and they hugged each other warmly. His mother had her back to him and was chomping on a stick of bamboo. Remembering what a scene he'd made yesterday morning when he'd stomped out of the clearing, Ping tiptoed up behind her and spoke softly in her ear.

"I'm sorry I was rude to you," he said. "Can you forgive me?"

His mother turned around, startled by the sound of his voice.

"Ping!" she gasped, letting the stick of bamboo fall from her mouth. She jumped to her feet and wrapped him up in a giant hug. "Where have you been, you naughty boy? I've been so worried about you. You missed supper, you know!"

"Sorry," Ping muttered sheepishly for the second time.

"What have you been up to?" she asked, pushing him away from her so that she could check him for cuts and bruises. "You haven't been doing anything dangerous, have you?"

Ping suddenly found himself faced with a choice. He could tell his mother the truth, about the rushing river, the roaring waterfall, the scary forest, the bandits, and the snow leopard that wanted to eat him, or he could save her some worry and tell her a little white lie instead.

"It wasn't a dangerous day at all," Ping said calmly. "In fact, as days-out go, I'd say it was rather boring."

And that, as Ping well knew, was exactly what his mother wanted to hear.

Later that day, after a leisurely breakfast in bed, Ping, his mother, Mao Mao, and his twin sister, An, retired to lounge on their backs on a bed of rhododendron leaves, chewing bamboo and spotting cloud shapes in the sky.

"Frog," said An lazily.

"Chicken," said Mao Mao.

"Snow leopard," said Ping.

"Where?" asked his twin sister.

"Can you see the cloud that looks like the tall ranger's hat?"

An nodded.

"It's next to that."

"How do you know what a snow leopard looks like?" asked his mother, eyeing Ping suspiciously. "I thought I was the only one who'd seen one. Or am I wrong?"

"Hui told me," lied Ping, speedily covering his tracks.

There was a long silence while his mother stripped a leaf from her bamboo stick and chewed it seventy-two times before swallowing.

"So after yesterday," she said at last, "would you say you've learned your lesson?"

"Which lesson's that?" he asked.

"The wise panda searches not for what he does not have, but is content with what is his."

"Yes. I would definitely say I've learned that lesson," said Ping.

"And the other?"

"Was there another?" he asked.

"Master the art of boredom, and you will conquer the world," she reminded him.

"Done that too," he said. "I can be bored silly now and it doesn't bother me at all."

"Good," said his mother. "So you won't be going off on another big adventure soon, then?"

Ping smiled a knowing smile to himself as his thoughts wandered. And while he dreamed of exploits yet to come, somewhere in the background his mother's distant voice called out, "Ping. You haven't answered me... Ping? Ping! PING!"